W9-AUZ-019

W9-CEK-885
Discard

What Kind of Baby-sitter Is This?

written and illustrated by Dolores Johnson

Macmillan Publishing Company New York
Collier Macmillan Canada Toronto
Maxwell Macmillan International Publishing Group
New York Oxford Singapore Sydney

Macmillan Publishing Company
866 Third Avenue, New York, NY 10022
Collier Macmillan Canada, Inc.
1200 Eglinton Avenue East, Suite 200
Don Mills, Ontario M3C 3N1
First edition   Printed in Hong Kong

10 9 8 7 6 5 4 3 2 1

The text of this book is set in 15 point ITC Zapf International Light.
The illustrations are rendered in watercolor and colored pencil on paper.
Library of Congress Cataloging-in-Publication Data
Johnson, Dolores. What kind of babysitter is this?
/ written and illustrated by Dolores Johnson.
— 1st ed.   p.   cm.
Summary: Kevin intensely dislikes the idea of having
a babysitter, until the unconventional baseball-loving
“Aunt” Lovey arrives to change his mind.
ISBN 0-02-747846-7
[1. Babysitters—Fiction.] I. Title.
PZ7.J631635Wf 1991 [E]—dc20
90-42860 CIP AC

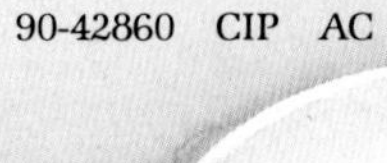

To those who have helped me:

Nina Kidd
Deborah N. Lattimore
Kendra Marcus
Cecilia Yung

Kevin's mother was getting all dressed up to go out. And then the doorbell rang.

"Not another baby-sitter!" cried Kevin. "You said you'd take me with you next time!

If you leave me tonight I . . . I . . . I . . .
I'm not going to be your friend!"

“Kevin,” said his mother. “This is Mrs. Lovey Pritchard. She’ll take care of you while I’m away at school.”

"Take a look at that face, that sweet little face," said the baby-sitter. "You can call me Aunt Lovey, sugar dumpling."

"Mom, take me with you!" yelled Kevin.

"So you're the little boy who doesn't like baby-sitters," said Aunt Lovey. "Well, we're going to have such fun together."

"Mom, don't leave me with her, puullleeease!" yelled Kevin.

"Don't you worry about us, little mother," said the baby-sitter. "Kevin and I will be just fine."

"Well, I'm leaving, too!" said Kevin as he stormed through the kitchen out to the back porch. "That old lady will never miss me. She'll be busy doing what baby-sitters do—painting her toenails, talking on the telephone, and eating the good stuff in the refrigerator. Hey, she'd better not eat that last piece of cake!"

Kevin sneaked back into the kitchen. "Isn't she even gonna come after me? Is that lady so dumb she doesn't even know I'm gone?"

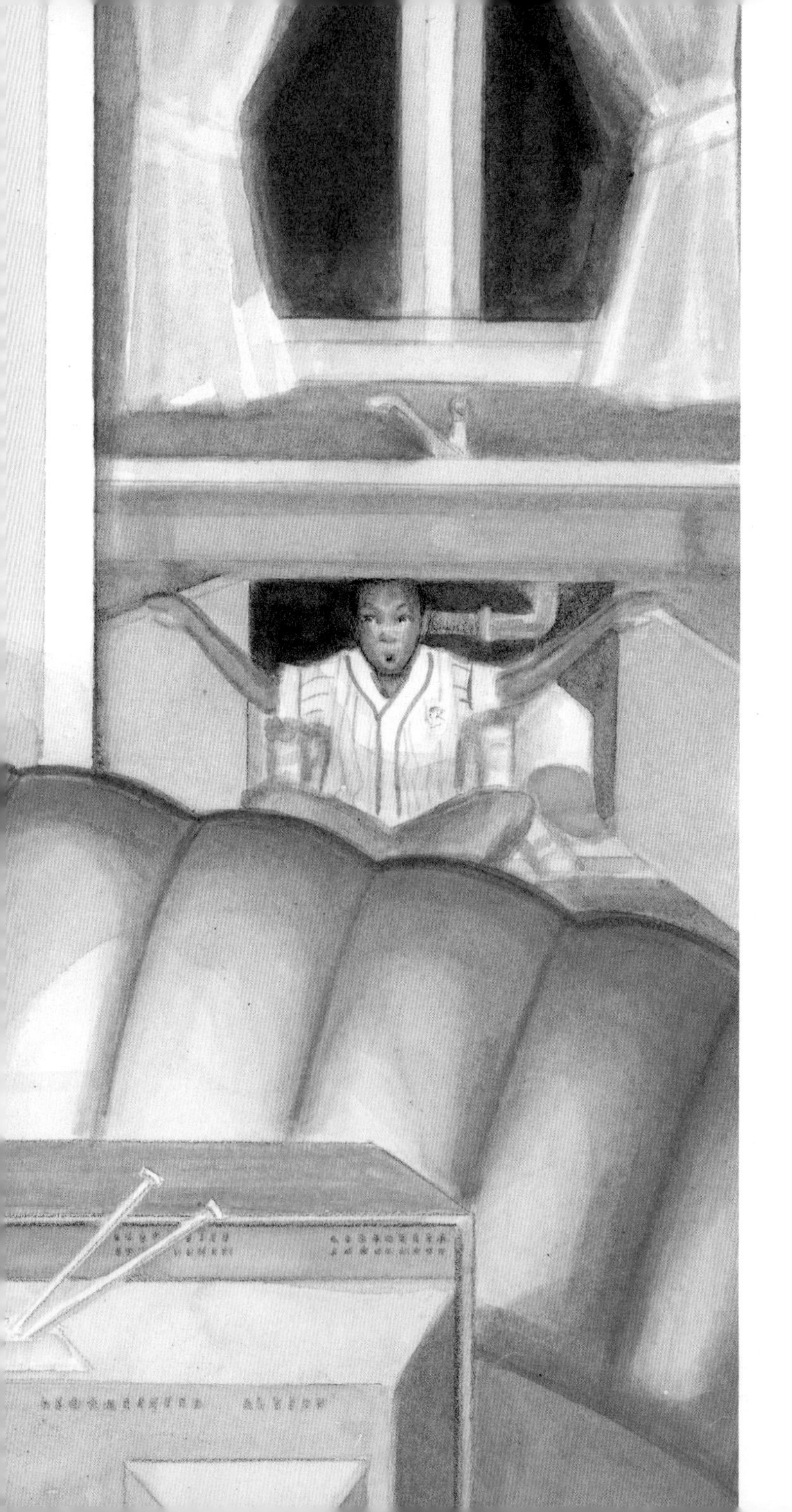

From his hiding place, Kevin heard the click of a switch and then the roar of the television. "So that's what she's doing. She's watching soap operas. And my mom is paying her a zillion dollars to watch *me*."

Aunt Lovey started yelling, jumping up and down, and clapping. "She's watching my baseball game! My *mom* wouldn't even watch it. What kind of baby-sitter is this? She's supposed to be yelling at *me*."

B

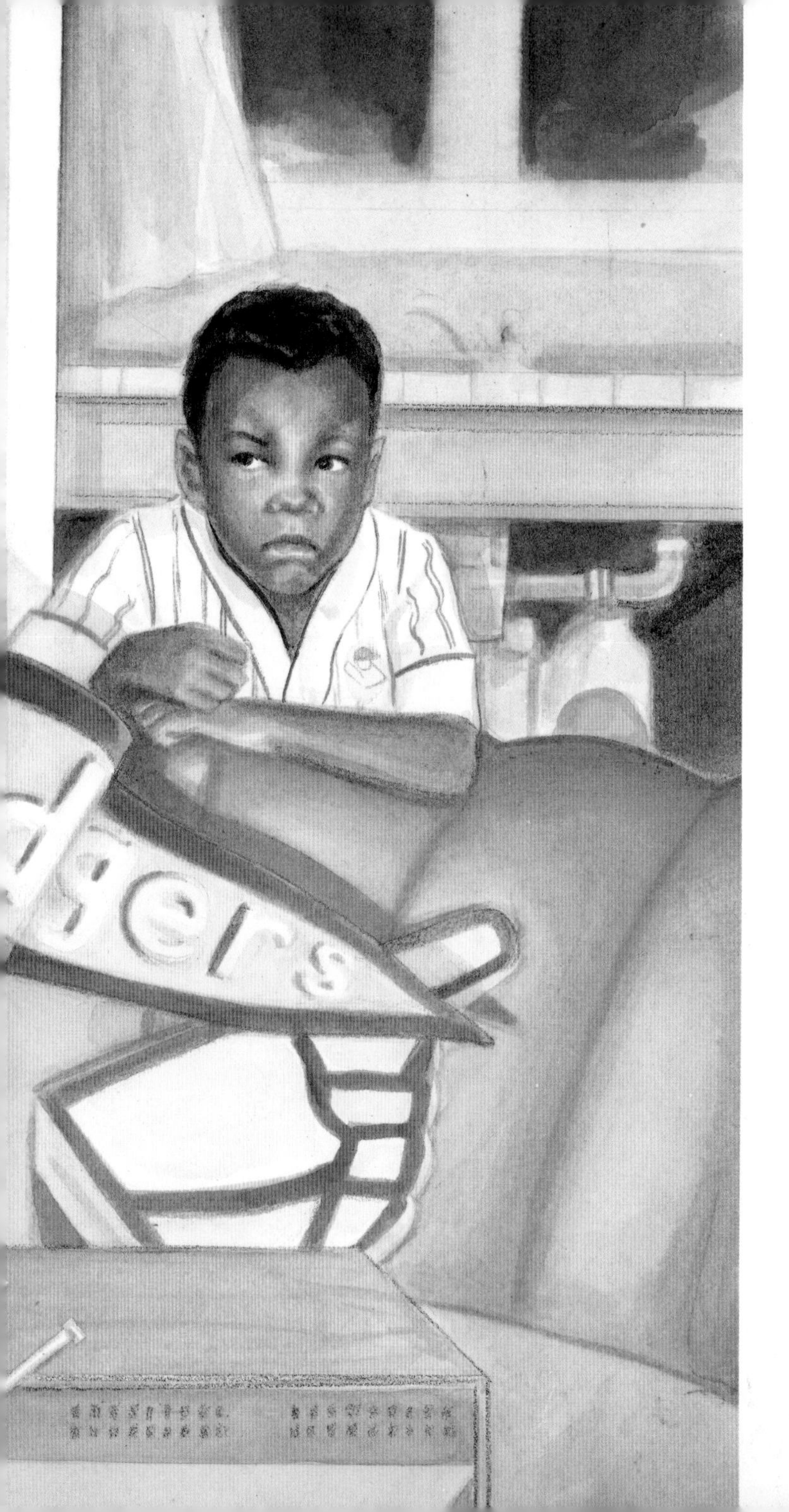

The baby-sitter started pulling things from her handbag. She put a baseball cap on her head. She laid some baseball cards on the couch, and she waved a pennant in the air.

"I wish she would put that pennant down," said Kevin. "I can hardly see."

"And it's a Badger pennant," continued Kevin. "That proves it. She doesn't know anything about baseball. Everybody knows that the Badgers can't win."

When the ball game ended, and the Badgers had won, Aunt Lovey turned off the television set. She was so busy pulling things out of her purse, it seems she never even noticed Kevin.

"Oh, no," said Kevin. "Here it comes now... her telephone numbers . . . her nail polish . . . those kissy-kissy books that baby-sitters read."

But Aunt Lovey pulled out a book about baseball, opened it, and began to read softly.

"I wish she would speak up," said Kevin. "I can hardly hear."

So Kevin crawled closer and Aunt Lovey read louder, and they read, and played games, and told jokes, and laughed so much that they didn't even notice when Kevin's mother came home.

"Are you still angry with me, sweetheart?" Kevin's mother asked when she came in. "I really hated to leave you. But, of course, there'll be other times when I'll have to go out."

"Well, that's all right, Mom, 'cause I've got a great idea," said Kevin. "Can Aunt Lovey move in with us? We can make her a bed on the couch, or she can share your bedroom with you. This can be her home, too."

"But, Kevin," said his mother, "Aunt Lovey has her own home. Baby-sitters don't stay over."

"Mom, you don't understand. Aunt Lovey's no baby-sitter—she's my friend!"